NORTHUMBERLAND COUNTY LIBRARY

Please return this book on or before the last date stamped below unless an extension of the loan period is granted.

Application for renewal may be made by letter or telephone.

Fines at the approved rate will be charged when a book is overdue.

FOR THE ORANGUTAN FOUNDATION –
FOR ALL THE GREAT WORK THEY
DO IN HELPING TO SAVE THESE
WONDERFUL CREATURES – JB & SV

STRIPES PUBLISHING
An imprint of Magi Publications
1 The Coda Centre, 189 Munster Road,
London SW6 6AW

A paperback original
First published in Great Britain in 2009

Text copyright © Jan Burchett and Sara Vogler, 2009
Illustrations copyright © Diane Le Feyer of Cartoon Saloon, 2009
Cover illustration copyright © Andrew Hutchinson, 2009

ISBN: 978-1-84715-066-0

WILD RESCUE

RESCUE

FOREST FIRE

Stripes

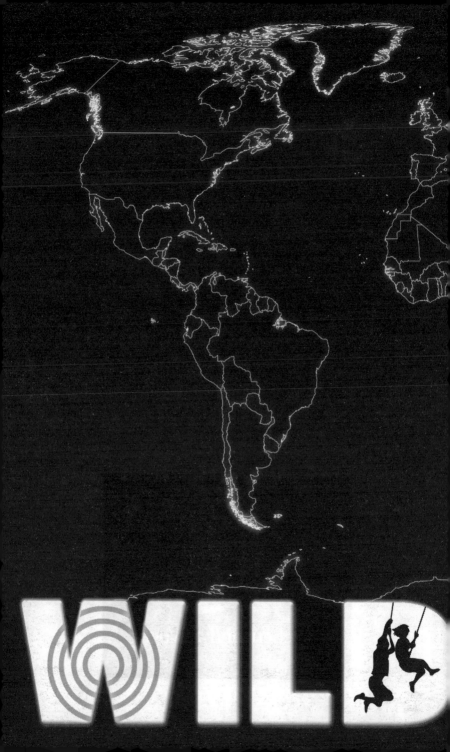

STATUS: FILE CLOSED
LOCATION:
SICHUAN, CHINA
CODE NAME: JING JING

STATUS: LIVE
LOCATION:
SOUTH BORNEO
CODE NAME: KAWAN

STATUS: FILE CLOSED
LOCATION:
SUMATRA, INDONESIA
CODE NAME: TORA

RESCUE
MISSION DATABASE

CHAPTER ONE

"Ready?" yelled Ben, pointing at the huge wave rolling towards them.

His twin sister Zoe grinned. "Ready!" Lying flat on her surfboard she began to paddle with her hands, getting up speed as the swell approached. When they felt the wave lift them, they jumped up and whizzed towards the shore, arms outstretched. They were having a great week staying at Gran's cottage by the sea.

"Awesome," exclaimed Ben, gathering up his board. "I felt like a killer shark!"

Zoe looked at him in his shiny purple wetsuit, his brown hair sticking up in salty spikes. "A killer grape more like!" she laughed.

"Ben! Zoe!"

They looked up the beach to where Gran was waving at them and pointing out to sea.

They turned to see a sleek catamaran slicing towards them. A blonde woman was at the helm.

"It's Erika!" gasped Ben, as they watched the cat spin to a sudden halt, sending spray into the air. "Looks like we're off on another Wild adventure!"

Ben and Zoe's parents were international vets and wherever their work took them the children usually went too. But this September they would be starting secondary school, so they had to stay in England with their gran for the summer. They'd been expecting six dull weeks until their godfather, Dr Stephen Fisher, had got in touch and recruited them into Wild, his top-secret organization dedicated to saving endangered animals. Their grandmother was the only other person who knew about it.

Yelling goodbye to Gran, they swam out towards the catamaran. Erika Bohn, Uncle Stephen's second-in-command, stretched out a hand and helped them up the ladder.

"It's good to see you again," Erika shouted, as they sped across the waves. "Dr Fisher is really pleased with your work for Wild. This time he's trusting you with a particularly difficult task, but as usual he wants to tell you himself."

She handed Zoe an envelope. "Here's your clue."

Zoe tipped up the envelope and a glass eyeball fell into her hand. She showed it to Ben.

"Deep brown iris," he said, inspecting it closely. "Looks almost human – except the white's quite dark."

Zoe peered at it. "Do you think it's one of the apes? That would be so cool."

She knew what to do next. She looked at the catamaran's control panel and located a small hole next to the radar screen.

"Let's find out," she said, slipping the eyeball in.

"Greetings, godchildren!" came a voice, and the hologram of a man appeared in front of them. He wore a baseball cap over his thick red hair and his shirt hung over his trousers.

"Oh, good, Uncle Stephen!" said Zoe. "Eccentric as ever."

"Ready for your next Wild mission?" asked the man. Then he chuckled. "I don't know why I'm asking — of course you are. Never had such able operatives as you two! Well, there's an orang-utan in trouble in Borneo. Tell you more when you get to HQ."

Uncle Stephen gave a cheery wave and disappeared.

Zoe sighed. "An orang-utan. Wow! They're such lovely, gentle creatures."

"And so endangered," added Ben. "Did you know that—"

"Their habitat is threatened by logging?" interrupted Zoe.

"I was going to say—"

"That they can use sign language? I knew that, too."

"No. I was about to say that they're more intelligent than you," said Ben, ducking away from her friendly shove with a grin.

Ben and Zoe gazed over the rough water as a small island came into view. There were a few buildings scattered about a ramshackle farm, with chickens pecking on the scrubby land. Erika brought down the sail and steered the cat deep into the gloom underneath a battered old jetty that looked as if it hadn't been used for years. As they climbed the waiting ladder, she pressed a remote and the craft glided forwards into a boat shed set in the bank.

Ben and Zoe knew the routine by now. They made for the tumbledown outside toilet, Erika at their heels. Ben bolted the door and Zoe pulled the chain.

Whoosh! The cubicle turned into a lift and shot deep into the earth.

"Who needs a rollercoaster when we've got Uncle Stephen's turbo toilet!" Ben laughed, clutching his belly.

Zoe and Erika followed Ben along a well-lit corridor to the Control Room. They placed their fingertips on an ID pad.

"Print identification complete," announced the electronic voice.

They burst into a bright room full of flashing control panels and computer screens – the nerve centre of Wild HQ. A pair of plimsolled feet was sticking out from under a console.

"Uncle Stephen," called Zoe softly.

There was a thump and a muffled curse, then the gangly figure of their godfather emerged, rubbing his head.

"Hello there," he said cheerfully. "Just fixing the phase converters. I've got the whole place running on solar power now." He looked at their wetsuits. "I know you're going to the *rain*forest, but it won't be that wet!"

"I picked Ben and Zoe up from the beach," explained Erika.

"Let me tell you about your mission." Uncle Stephen grinned. He touched a plasma screen and brought up a satellite map of a large island. "Borneo," he announced. "There was once a huge rainforest here, but there's been a lot of logging over the last few years – legal and illegal."

"I've read all about that," said Ben. "They're clearing the land for oil palm plantations. Palm oil's used all over the world – in margarine, soap, candles, cosmetics – loads of things."

"Mr Know-it-all." Zoe raised her eyebrows. "But you're right. The rainforest's disappearing really fast. Is that something to do with the orang-utan in danger?"

"Spot on, Zoe," said her godfather. "We've had reports from one of our operatives out there about an orang-utan called Kawan. Until recently he was living safely on the Adilah Reservation. But then suddenly he left his territory."

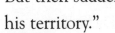

"Mat Ginting, who runs the reservation, had reared him from a baby," Erika explained. "He reintroduced Kawan into the wild last year."

"Orang-utans don't become independent until they're about seven or eight, do they?" said Ben. "No other animal in the world stays with its mother that long."

"You're correct, Ben," said Dr Fisher. "Kawan's about eight now. He had initially adapted well to living in the wild and had established his own territory. Male orang-utans live alone and their territory is very important to them. The only time they come near to other orang-utans is for mating or to fight another male who's strayed into their space."

"But then two weeks ago, there was some illegal logging in his area," said Erika. "Some men came at night and cut down several trees before they were chased off.

Wood is valuable and they intended to sell it. One of the felled trees had an orang-utan nest made of leaves that were still fresh, so Kawan must have been sleeping there. He fled in terror and hasn't been back since."

"So he's completely disappeared?" said Zoe.

"There have been a couple of sightings outside the reservation on a nearby oil palm plantation." Uncle Stephen took up the story. "But he hasn't wanted to come back to his territory. Now this is serious. Kawan is essential for Mr Ginting's dream of increasing the orang-utan population. There are very few males on the reservation."

"And orang-utans breed very slowly, don't they?" said Ben.

Uncle Stephen nodded. "A female may only have two or three babies in her whole lifetime." He pressed the screen again and a photo of a smiling young Bornean with black hair appeared. "Here's Mat Ginting. He set up the reservation ten years ago to help preserve the rainforest and its endangered inhabitants."

"He must be very brave," said Zoe. "I read that there are a lot of people who'll do anything to snatch rainforest land."

"Indeed, Zoe," agreed Dr Fisher. "Mat's one in a million. He's been running the reservation against all the odds, but money's becoming increasingly tight so he's going to start taking paying visitors."

"Apparently there's a grand opening in a few days," Erika added, "which is perfect timing for us. Tourists will be able to stay there and see orang-utans in their natural habitat."

"So you want us to pose as visitors to the reservation, locate Kawan and bring him back to his home?" asked Ben.

Dr Fisher nodded. "Of course, Mat Ginting mustn't know about our organization. And that's why you two are perfect for the job. He's unlikely to suspect a couple of kids."

"We're pretending you've won a competition by writing about endangered wildlife," said Erika.

"Erika's idea." Uncle Stephen beamed. "And a very good one."

"We've told Mr Ginting that the prize was a trip to a sanctuary in Brunei," Erika continued, "but unfortunately the people there had to cancel at the last minute because of illness. We asked if he could take you instead and he was delighted. In fact, you're going to be his very first guests."

"So you need to be on your way," said Uncle Stephen eagerly.

"What about our BUGs?" Ben reminded him.

"Of course!" Their godfather handed over what looked like two games consoles. The Brilliant Undercover Gizmos had a lot of useful functions: working as communicators, scent dispersers, translators and much more.

"I've invented a new gadget especially for this mission," said Dr Fisher, passing over a belt and pair of boots each. "Inside the boots there is the EEL – the Electronic Escape Line – a top-of-the-range bungee cord to prevent an over-speedy descent."

"In other words, it will save you if you're falling from a height!" explained Erika. "And you may be spending a lot of time in the trees in Borneo. All you need to do to activate it is press the silver button on the belt. Now, time to get you out of those wetsuits!"

"Hope you get Kawan back," called Uncle Stephen, diving back under the console.

"You can count on us!" declared Ben.

CHAPTER TWO

Erika drove the hired jeep through a pair of wooden gates and parked in a bare earth courtyard.

Bright, new wooden buildings joined to form two sides of the square. The whole courtyard was hung with colourful bunting and flags. Trees lined the fourth side and towered over the roofs all around, as if the rainforest was just waiting to take back this little space.

"The Adilah Reservation," announced Ben. "We're here!"

He and Zoe jumped out of the car and gasped in the humid afternoon heat after the cool of the car's air-conditioning. Insects buzzed overhead and they could hear exotic bird and animal cries from the forest. Two workers were fixing a banner over the entrance of one of the buildings. It read: "Grand Opening Today". Another man came over eagerly to greet them. He was carrying a hammer and nails, and a heavy sign. They recognized him from the photo they'd seen.

"Hello there! You must be Ben and Zoe!" He put down his tools and sign and shook the children's hands enthusiastically. "I'm Mat Ginting. Welcome to my reservation."

"It's great to be here," said Zoe with a beaming smile.

Erika took their backpacks from the boot. "We're so grateful you agreed to take on our winners," she said to Mat. "I'll pick them up at the end of their stay. Enjoy your prize, Ben and Zoe."

"Thank you, Miss Bohn," they replied politely. The children knew they mustn't show that she was anything more than the organizer of the competition. They also knew that Erika was heading off north to check out reports of more illegal logging.

Zoe looked at the sign Mat had been carrying. She'd seen the design on the journey. It was a huge "O" encircling a globe and supported by caring hands. They'd passed field after field where the

forest had been cleared for oil palm trees.
Every one of them had displayed this sign.

"Whose logo is that?" asked Zoe. "We
kept seeing it on the way here."

"Ostrander Industries," Mat told her.
"Pieter Ostrander, the owner, has been very
generous in giving donations to help us with
our work. The least we could do is put up his
plantation logo in time for the ceremony.
He's promised to make a speech for us."

"But isn't his plantation threatening the rainforest?" asked Ben. "It's taken over a huge area. We drove for several miles seeing nothing but his oil palms."

"And they're not even a native tree of Borneo!" burst in Zoe.

"We have to keep a balance," said Mat. "The plantation gives jobs to the locals *and* the forest must be preserved. That's why I took this land and I'll keep it safe. When Pieter first bought the plantation a few years ago he approached me and asked if I would sell him my reservation, but as soon as I told him what I was doing, he became very supportive. In fact, I've just had trouble with illegal logging in the east of my land. Pieter lent me some men to patrol the area and the loggers haven't been back since. Pieter's a good friend."

"Greetings!" called a voice.

A smiling young woman came out of one

of the buildings. A baby orang-utan clung
to her neck, its head against her shoulder.
It had soft orange hair and a round, baby
belly. It looked solemnly at the children.

"My name is Yasmin," said the woman,
pushing her long, dark fringe out of her
eyes. "I am Mat's wife. And you must be the
competition winners. Congratulations."

"Thank you," said Ben with a grin.

"Who's this?" asked Zoe, stroking the soft
fur of the baby orang-utan. It grabbed her
finger and held it. Zoe couldn't help letting
out a happy sigh.

"His name is Biza," said Yasmin fondly. "He is an orphan we are caring for. We cannot resist a baby who needs help. They go back into the wild when they are old enough."

"But they do come back to see us," added Mat. "Orang-utans make a bond with their primary carer. Some of the females show us their babies as if we were grandparents!"

"And we are just as proud!" laughed Yasmin. "Come. Biza and I will show you your bedroom and you can unpack. In an hour we have our opening ceremony."

Ben and Zoe breathed in the welcoming smell of new wood as they followed her through a kitchen with a huge table to a corridor of bedrooms.

"These are the guest quarters," she announced. "When you are ready Mat will be waiting for you in his office. It is across the courtyard."

Left alone in their cool bedroom with its two beds and shower room, Ben and Zoe quickly emptied their backpacks of everything but their essential Wild equipment. Zoe detached the translator earpiece from her BUG and stuck it into her ear.

"Don't forget yours, Ben," she said. "We want to understand everything people are saying, even when they're speaking Malay."

The children found Mat sitting in an office, working at an old-fashioned computer.

"I'm updating my records while I have a chance," he told them, as he handed them a welcome drink of iced juice. "I make daily entries about our orang-utans ... well, all but one."

"Why not all?" Zoe made it sound like a casual enquiry.

Ben grinned to himself. His sister wasn't wasting time in finding out information for their mission.

"One of our orang-utans has left the reservation," Mat told them. "He's a young male called Kawan. He's been with us since he was tiny. He was taken from his mother by poachers who were going to sell him as a pet to some rich westerner!"

"That's awful!" gasped Zoe.

"Luckily, they were arrested in time and Kawan was brought to me," Mat went on. "I had no idea where he'd come from so I couldn't find his mother. He was the first orang-utan I raised from a baby."

He sighed, a wistful look on his face. "I released him into the wild last year. But he still came by every morning for a rusk. Until two weeks ago, that is. He hasn't been back since the logging scared him off."

"Is he more wary of humans than other orang-utans are because of what happened when he was little?" asked Ben.

"It seems that way," said Mat. "At least I know he's alive. One of my staff, Daud, sighted him on Mr Ostrander's oil palm plantation at the edge of the reservation when he was working on the walkway."

He grinned at them. "Would you like to see some footage of Kawan doing his jungle training? It's me showing him how to look after himself – being his mother in a way. I'm sure we have time before the ceremony."

"Yes please," said Ben and Zoe together.

Mat took them through into a larger room where log benches faced a screen. He gestured for them to sit. "You're the first guests to see this," he said. "Daud filmed it. He's very fond of Kawan, too." The screen flashed into life and the words "Adilah Reservation" appeared. Mat fast-forwarded to a scene where he was teaching a tiny orang-utan how to climb a tree. The solemn little ape had a comical tuft of light hair sticking up on one side of his head. He was faithfully copying Mat's every move until Mat made a strange chirruping noise.

"Kawan always comes to that call," explained Mat. "At least he did. Now he must be too far away to hear it. When the official opening is over and we're all back to normal I'm going to go and find him. Pieter let me have a look on the plantation before, but I haven't had the chance to do a thorough search. The plantation's not a natural home for an orang-utan – and I fear he must be eating the young oil palm seedlings. That's not fair on Pieter."

They watched the footage of young Kawan responding to Mat's call by abandoning his task, climbing on Mat's head and clinging to his ears.

"Ahhh," said Ben. "How cute. Do show it again."

Zoe looked at him, puzzled. It wasn't like her brother to go gooey over animals. That was her job!

But as the film replayed she glimpsed him slip out his BUG and hit a button. Now she knew what he was up to. He was recording Mat's call. She smiled to herself. If they could get to Kawan's old territory, they could play the recording through the digital super-amplifier on the BUG. Hopefully the orang-utan would hear it and come home.

CHAPTER THREE

"Look at all that food!" exclaimed Ben, staring hungrily at the feast spread out on tables in the courtyard. "I'm ready for my lunch."

"You'll have to wait till after the speeches," hissed Zoe. "The opening ceremony's about to begin."

Ben and Zoe were standing with Mat and Yasmin – and Biza – at the front of a large crowd of locals, waiting for Pieter Ostrander to arrive. A reporter was already taking photos of the new buildings.

One of the workers they'd seen when they arrived was putting jugs of drink on the table. He smiled at Ben and sneaked him a piece of bread.

Ben tried to nibble it without being seen. "Thanks!" he said gratefully. "I'm sorry, I don't know your name."

"I'm Daud," said the young man. He pointed to the other man who'd been helping him earlier. He was older, with greying hair, and stood on his own in the middle of the crowd. "And that is Talib. We work for Mat."

Ben and Zoe were just introducing themselves when there was the roar of an engine and a sleek, sporty jeep drove through the gates. There was something large in the back, wrapped in brown paper. The jeep came to a halt and a tall, tanned man in smart, well-pressed trousers stepped out, beaming at everyone.

Mat brought him through the crowd. "Come and meet our competition winners, Pieter," he said as they approached the children. "Ben and Zoe, this is Mr Ostrander."

"I've heard all about you," said Pieter Ostrander. "Well done! So what did you do to make sure yours was the best entry?"

Zoe felt Ben's eyes on her. They realized they hadn't worked out a story.

36

"We … um … wrote an essay on…" she began.

"…the problems facing the Giant Panda in the wild," finished Ben.

That was clever, thought Zoe. They knew a lot about pandas – and how to rescue them!

"Fascinating," said Mr Ostrander. "It's good to see young people like you taking such an interest in endangered species."

"Mat has told us all about you, too, Mr Ostrander," said Ben. "He explained how much your company has helped him with the reservation."

"Just doing a neighbour a good turn," said Mr Ostrander. "We both have the same values. We want to protect what we have."

"I think we're ready now, Pieter," said Mat. He called for silence. "Thank you for coming here today for the Grand Opening Ceremony of the Adilah Reservation!

Mr Ostrander will now say a few words."
He spoke first in Malay and then in English
for Ben and Zoe. The children gave each
other a glance. Little did Mat know that
their earpieces were translating every word.

Mr Ostrander turned to the assembled
crowd.

"We are here today to open this
wonderful place and I would like to say a
few words to honour the man who made it
all possible – Mat Ginting."

Mat bent his head and shuffled his feet
in embarrassment as Mr Ostrander sang
his praises.

"And in conclusion," Mr Ostrander said,
"I declare the Adilah Reservation open for
business." He walked over to his jeep. "Now
if your men could give me a hand," he said.
"I've got a present for you."

Mat spoke over his shoulder in Malay
and Talib and Daud went over to the jeep.

They helped Mr Ostrander lift out the large, bulky package. It looked as if it was very heavy. Mr Ostrander cut the string and pulled away the paper. Everyone gasped as a wooden statue of an orang-utan was revealed. The reporter stepped forward and took pictures.

"It's wonderful!" exclaimed Mat, stroking the polished wood. "It will have pride of place by the gates."

"Now eat, everyone!" laughed Yasmin, pointing to the tables.

Ben didn't wait to be asked twice.

As Ben and Zoe piled their plates with food, Mat came over.

"When this is all over, I'll take you out into the reservation," he said. "There'll be time before nightfall."

"Awesome!" declared Ben, giving Zoe a secret thumbs up.

They each knew what the other was thinking. They were going to make sure that Mat took them to Kawan's old territory.

CHAPTER FOUR

The ceremony and meal were over at last, and Ben and Zoe sat in the shade of the reservation courtyard. Ben fidgeted impatiently.

"Sit still!" Zoe poked her brother in the ribs. "Mat said he'd be here at four o'clock, the moment he's said goodbye to all his guests. It's not even five to yet."

"I know, but I can't wait," groaned Ben, jumping up to look at the map displayed on the wall behind them. "A guided tour on walkways right up in the trees, with viewing platforms all along the way. So cool!"

"Don't forget – we're here for Kawan," Zoe reminded him. "We've got to find out all we can."

"I haven't forgotten," said Ben indignantly. "I've got the recording all ready to play if we get the chance to be on our own."

"Ready?" came an eager voice.

Mat was back. He handed them each a pair of binoculars and a paper bag. "There are rusks for the orang-utans in here. They love them."

He led them along a narrow pathway through the trees. At the sound of their footsteps shrill, harsh warning cries could be heard.

"Proboscis monkeys," explained Mat. "Very excitable." He stopped at a huge climbing frame of reddish wood where a ladder led up to a high, railed platform.

"What are we waiting for?" said Ben, grabbing the rungs.

"Great to see you're so keen, Ben," said Mat. "I expect this is the first time you'll actually come face to face with real wild animals."

Ben and Zoe just smiled.

"Don't forget, if any animal gets close, just stay quiet and calm. We're sure to come across some orang-utans. They're peaceable creatures – and very nosy. They'll probably come to you. The walkways are secure and every platform has an escape ladder down to the ground. Enough safety talk. Let's climb!"

"I wish we could catch sight of … what was the name of the young orang-utan that's gone missing?" Zoe asked innocently, as they reached the top of the ladder and stepped on to the platform. A walkway made of slats of wood fixed on long ropes stretched away into the distance.

"Kawan," said Mat. "We'll head for the area that used to be his territory. I keep hoping he'll be there."

Mat stepped on to the walkway, grasping the handrails. It swayed gently under his weight. The children followed him eagerly along the aerial path from tree to tree.

Above the harsh
croaking of frogs, macaques
screeched as they swung
from tree to tree and parrots
shrieked from nearby branches.
At each platform there were
information boards about the
creatures to look out for. Ben
studied each one.

"What are those?" asked
Zoe, pointing at some odd-
looking birds perched above
their heads. "Looks as if they've
got horns on their beaks."

"Didn't you read the sign?"
Ben teased. "They're rhinoceros
birds. What a fantastic place this is."

"Yasmin and I are trying to make this
a perfect haven for the animals," said
Mat. "The rainforest might be shrinking,
but this bit's not going to."

There was a loud rustling of leaves and suddenly two orang-utans burst into view, swinging after each other across the interwoven branches.

"Your first glimpse of orang-utans in the wild," Mat told them. "That's Lola and Kiki. They're mother and daughter. They'll come and say hello in a minute."

The two apes suddenly stopped their play as they spotted the humans. With a terrified shriek they turned and disappeared amongst the dense trees.

"Did we scare them away?" asked Zoe, disappointed.

"I don't think so," said Mat frowning. "But I'm surprised they left so quickly. They're usually very friendly. They even sat with us and tried out our tools when we were building the walkways." He stopped and looked around. The children could see the concern on his face.

"Come to think of it, it's been quieter than usual today. We've been through several territories and only seen Lola and Kiki." He led them round a platform, down a ladder and on to a lower walkway. "We're just coming into Kawan's old patch now."

Ben gave Zoe a thumbs up. Maybe they'd learn something useful here.

The walkway took them alongside a wide, muddy coloured river.

"This is the Munia River," Mat told them.

"Those are oil palms growing on the other side, aren't they?" asked Zoe, recognizing the straight rows of low-growing trees. They looked very different from the natural tangle of the high rainforest.

"That's Mr Ostrander's land," said Mat. "We're right in the south-eastern corner of the reservation now."

He led them on to a wide platform hung from a thick-trunked tree. A metal sign reading "Platform Twenty-two" was fixed to the trunk above a map of the walkways. The children looked at the view. The river wound its way into the distance, separating the palm trees from a wide swathe of flat land, where small plants in metal drums were growing at regular intervals.

"New oil palms," Mat explained. "That's where Daud spotted Kawan. I've tried calling him from here, but I'm not sure the sound travels that far."

"I hope he comes back soon," said Zoe.

"I'd love you to meet Kawan," said Mat. "He's such a character, and a great imitator. He used to fill up pans with rice and beans and stir them with a spoon. Copying Yasmin cooking, you see. It might be no use, but I have to try calling him again."

He pursed his lips together and made the call the children had heard on the film.

Ben and Zoe walked round to the opposite side of the platform. From here they could see a bald area of tree stumps. It looked like an ugly gash in the middle of the dense rainforest.

"Those evil loggers," said Zoe, looking at the devastation. "I'm glad they were chased off before they did any more damage. Poor Kawan, he must have been so frightened by them."

"I wish I could play my recording," whispered Ben. "At full volume it would reach those oil palms and beyond. If Kawan is there, he'll hear it."

Mat stopped calling for Kawan and came to join them.

"No luck, I'm afraid," he said. He pointed to the damaged area. "Kawan always nests – or rather, nested – around there. Don't worry, he doesn't think he's a bird!" Mat grinned. "Orang-utans make themselves a different bed every night up in the tree canopy. They even use big leaves as duvets!"

Ben nodded. "I've read about that," he said.

"Sometimes they hold them as sunshades," Mat went on, "and—" He was interrupted by a shrill beeping from his shirt pocket. "Sorry about this," he said, pulling out a walkie-talkie. "It must be Yasmin back at the centre."

He turned away from the children, speaking rapidly in Malay.

"Something's wrong…" They heard Yasmin's reply translated through their earpieces. "…more cancellations. The Coopers."

"They were due next week, weren't they?" said Mat.

His walkie-talkie buzzed and Yasmin spoke again. "…lucky they emailed to find out when they could rebook … don't understand … cancellations have been sent out to our guests… How could that happen?"

"I'll come straight back," said Mat into the walkie-talkie. "We'll phone everyone and reinstate their bookings. Then we'll look into it. Probably something to do with that old dinosaur of a computer."

He ended the transmission and turned to Ben and Zoe. "Sorry," he said, in English. "We have to return now. Just a little problem with our guest bookings.

We'll come again tomorrow morning." He turned and headed back along the walkway towards the reservation.

"We'll follow in a second," Ben called after him. "I've just spotted a broadbill – must get a picture." He pulled Zoe to a halt.

"We haven't had a chance to play the recording," he muttered, as he aimed his camera at the bird.

"Then we come back tonight," said Zoe. "On our own."

CHAPTER FIVE

Zoe crept over the bare wooden floor of their bedroom and nudged her brother through his mosquito net.

"Wake up," she whispered. "We've got two hours until sunrise."

Ben opened his eyes and sat bolt upright in the dark. "Let's go."

They dressed quickly and put on their backpacks. They'd filled them the night before with water, their first aid kit and BUGs. Having put on their EEL belts and boots, they snatched up their night goggles.

Zoe slowly opened the door.

"Shhhh!" hissed Ben as the hinges groaned.

"Lucky there are no stairs," muttered Zoe. "It's bad enough in this creaky wooden corridor."

They stepped outside into the silent, shadowy compound. As soon as they put on their goggles the scene was bathed in green light. Deep puddles lay on the ground and they could hear water dripping from the trees.

"Looks like we've just missed a shower," whispered Ben.

Zoe turned a dial on the nosepiece to adjust the focus. "We'll follow the satellite map on the BUGs."

They crept for the cover of the trees.

"The black zigzag lines are the walkways," said Ben, studying the image on his BUG screen. "And there's Kawan's territory, where the walkways come to the river."

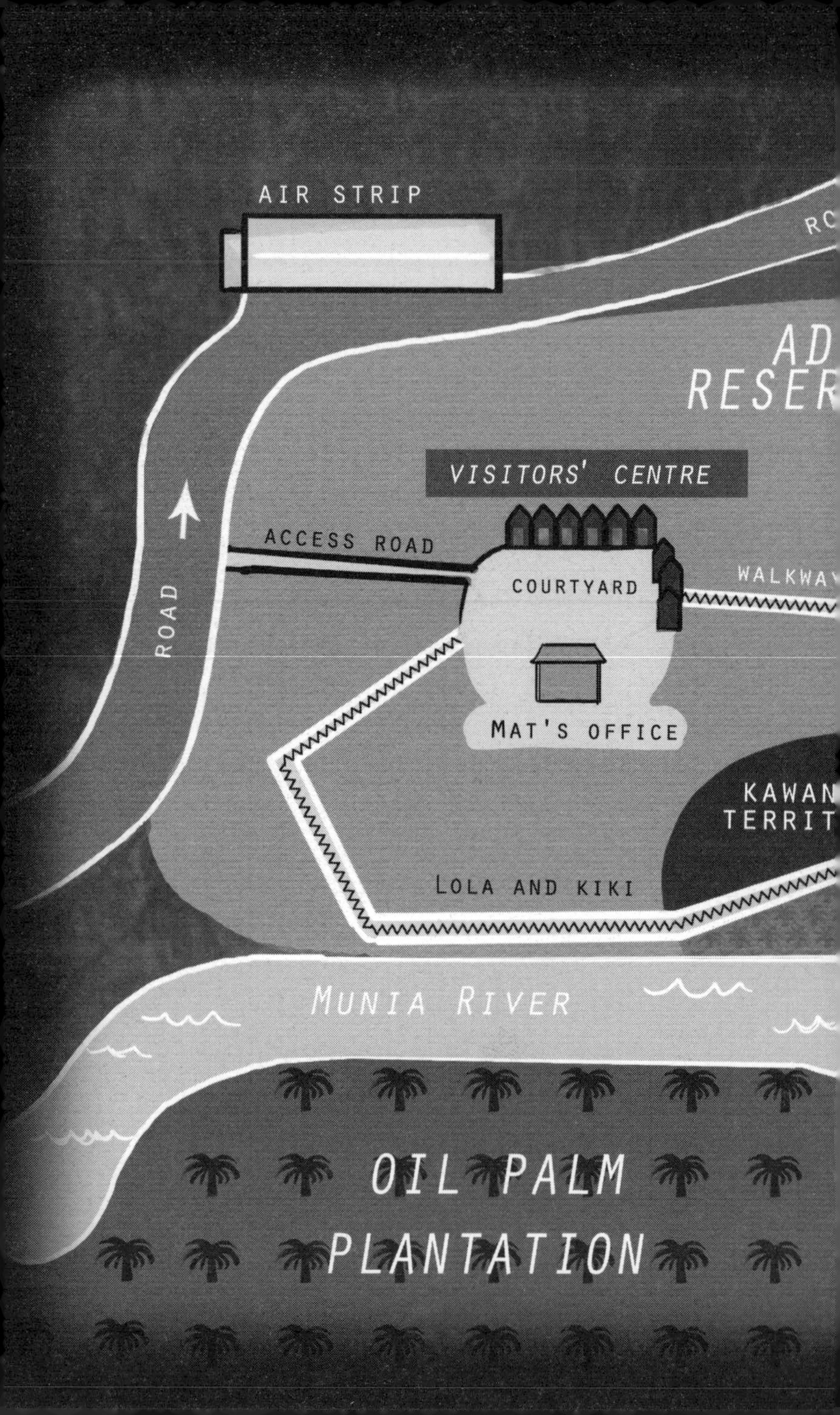
AIR STRIP
VISITORS' CENTRE
ACCESS ROAD
ROAD
COURTYARD
MAT'S OFFICE
LOLA AND KIKI
MUNIA RIVER
OIL PALM
PLANTATION

ION

OIL PALM
PLANTATION

NEW
SEEDLINGS

N

NOT TO SCALE

"There must be a more direct path than that," replied Zoe.

Ben pressed a button and a different map appeared, showing a narrow track that went right to the south-east edge of the reservation. "This'll take us there."

"Tuck your trousers into your boots," Zoe reminded him. "There'll be snakes."

"And arthropods and invertebrates," said Ben eagerly.

"Creepy-crawlies in other words." Zoe grimaced.

"Watch out for the ten-centimetre-long cockroaches!" Ben teased, but Zoe refused to rise to the bait.

"Scent dispersers on, too," she said. "That will help keep unwanted guests away."

The rough path led between huge, thick tree trunks deep into the darkness of the rainforest. The children moved along as quietly as they could, listening intently to the sounds around them.

Suddenly there was a loud *whoo-aa* call
and a long, skinny shape swung down in
front of them. It peered at them intently
from under a pair of thick eyebrows. The
children stopped dead, hearts beating fast.
Then the creature gave a cry and shot back
up into the trees.

"It was a gibbon!" whispered Zoe,
checking the analysis on her BUG.
"Wonder what it made of our goggled faces!"

"What's that?"
gasped Ben,
pointing
into the
darkness.
"Around
that trunk.
It looks
like a huge
snake!"

"It's not moving." Zoe laughed. "It's just a root that's twisted round the tree."

They pushed their way through a bank of thick fern leaves that hung across the path.

"I can hear the river," said Ben. "We must nearly be in Kawan's territory. The walkways ought to be above us now."

"There's a sign on that trunk," said Zoe pointing. "Platform Twenty-two – that's where we were earlier. We've arrived."

Something moved low on the ground ahead. Through their goggles they got a glimpse of cold reptilian eyes and a scaly snout edging towards them.

"Crocodile!" gasped Ben, pulling Zoe back. "We have to get off the ground – now!"

"But how?" Zoe looked round wildly.

"There'll be a ladder up to the platform." Ben stumbled through the ferns to reach the numbered trunk. Zoe was close on

his heels. Behind her the
ferns swayed and flattened
as the crocodile followed.

Ben leaped up the first
rungs of the wooden
ladder. He reached down
and grabbed Zoe's hand,
hauling her up to safety
just as the crocodile
launched itself at the base
of the tree, snapping at the
empty air beneath her feet.

"That was close!" breathed his sister, scrambling up as high as she could. "I thought we were safe with our scent dispersers on."

"Crocs have really acute hearing," Ben told her, as he looked down at the enormous scaly creature that was still searching for its prey. "We weren't exactly silent back there. Did you know," he went on, as they climbed towards the platform, "the saltwater crocodile can grow up to seven metres long?"

"Fascinating," panted Zoe, following on behind. "Plenty of room inside for a couple of kids then!"

At last they were on the platform. Down below they could see the distant shape of their attacker sliding back towards the dark sweep of the river that lay beyond the trees.

"This will be a good place to try the call," said Ben.

He pulled out his BUG and pressed

some buttons. A loud chirruping noise filled the air and echoed far into the trees.

"It would have been better to do this in the day when Kawan was awake," said Zoe.

"We've got no choice," Ben replied. "And I'm sure he'll forgive us if it means he comes home."

They sat as still as they could, carefully scanning the area through their goggles.

"Fruit bats, otters and one or two monkeys," reported Zoe. "I think they were silvered langurs. No orang-utans."

Ben played the call again and again.

"Looks like we're going to be unlucky," he said at last. "Perhaps we should be making our way back—"

He stopped. There was a rustling in the branches above their heads, followed by a loud chomping sound. Zoe quickly held out her BUG towards it to analyze the sound. "It's an orang-utan!" she whispered.

"I've read about their vocalizations," said Ben. "That sound means it feels threatened."

"Keep still then," said Zoe. "It has to be Kawan, doesn't it? He's responded to the call. And after all we're in his territory so none of the others would dare to be here."

"Goggles on zoom," Ben reminded her, adjusting his as he spoke.

"Wow!" murmured Zoe. "He's right above our heads."

A dark shape was stealing through the high branches.

Ben wriggled round and held his BUG above the leaves, activating its camera function. "Got a photo," he whispered. They peered down at the screen. The face of a familiar looking young orang-utan stared back at them. He had a distinctive tuft of hair sticking up on one side of his head, just like they'd seen in the film.

"Awesome!" breathed Ben. "It *is* Kawan!"

CHAPTER SIX

The young orang-utan sat in the branches above their heads, gazing at Ben and Zoe, his eyes flickering nervously.

"I've got a rusk in my backpack," Zoe said quietly. "Let's see if we can tempt him down and make him feel safe in his territory again."

"Mat's going to be so happy," said Ben.

Moving in ultra slow motion, Zoe stood up and held the rusk above her head.

Kawan began to swing gracefully down from branch to branch. He waited just out of reach, hanging from one long, shaggy arm and gazing around as if searching for somebody. He looked tense – ready to escape at the slightest threat.

"Do you think he's wondering where Mat is?" said Ben. "I hope he doesn't leave when he realizes Mat's not here."

"Come on, Kawan," said Zoe gently. "Here, boy." She waved the rusk.

Kawan hesitated, then extended one leathery hand and took the rusk. Eyes firmly fixed on them, he solemnly nibbled at the treat, dropping the crumbs around their feet.

"He still looks very nervous," said Ben. "Those loggers must have really scared him."

"I think we've got his trust or he wouldn't come so close," said Zoe, pulling out another rusk ready to hand to the young ape. "Something must be telling him we're OK. Maybe it was Mat's call."

Kawan put out a crumby finger and touched Zoe's cheek. Zoe sighed with delight.

"I can see why Mat's so fond of him. He's adorable."

Kawan dropped down on to the platform and reached out for the second rusk.

"Good boy, Kawan," whispered Ben.

At that moment, the sound of an explosion filled the air. Without thinking, the children threw themselves down on to the wooden slats.

With a terrified shriek Kawan was off, swinging away through the trees. Soon he was out of sight.

"Was that a gunshot?" Zoe said in horror.

"I don't think so," said Ben. "But I've heard that sort of sound before somewhere." He gripped her arm. "Someone's down there – heading through the undergrowth."

They peered down over the side of the slats. A shadowy figure was hurrying along the ground.

"It's a man," hissed Ben. "What's he doing here at this time of night?"

"Let's follow," said Zoe.

Moving swiftly along the swaying walkway, they followed the sound until they reached the next platform.

"This is where we saw Lola and Kiki," whispered Zoe. "The walkway after this is much higher, remember. There's a ladder somewhere here." She flinched as another sharp bang filled the air, followed by frightened animal cries. "What *is* that?"

Zoe found the top of the ladder and

climbed up to the next platform, feeling for each rung in the dark.

"Hurry," hissed Ben. "He's getting away."

Zoe didn't need telling twice. She set off ahead of her brother along the wobbly wooden slats of the new walkway.

CRACK! There was a loud splitting sound under her feet. She heard Ben's cry of alarm as she felt herself falling.

Zoe flung out her arms and grabbed desperately at the broken walkway. Her hands closed round a wooden slat and she felt her arms being almost jerked out of their sockets as she stopped falling. She gripped on with all her strength, not daring to look at the ground.

"Hold on," Ben called, trying to keep the panic out of his voice.

"I'm not planning on going anywhere," Zoe puffed. *Especially not down!* she thought to herself. She could just see Ben crouched

on the walkway, one hand reaching out to
pull her to safety.

Then something else caught her eye. The
ropes that supported the slatted walkway
were only holding by a single strand.

"Get back, Ben," she shouted. "The
whole thing's going to give way!"

There was a ripping sound as the last
strand of rope began to fray, and Zoe felt
herself jolting downwards, legs swinging.

Then the rope snapped and Zoe began
to fall.

CHAPTER SEVEN

Ben had a split second to react. He slammed the button on his belt and felt a cord shoot out from his boots towards the trees, as he dived off the platform. He grabbed hold of Zoe by the straps of her backpack and together they tumbled through the air.

For a second, a whirl of dark undergrowth flashed in front of their eyes as the ground came towards them at a dizzying speed.

Then suddenly they were jerked upwards again.

"Good old
Uncle Stephen!"
Ben yelled in Zoe's
ear. They finally
came to a halt dangling above the ground,
twisting slowly. "That certainly tested out
his EEL." Ben checked the terrain below.
"Not a crocodile in sight. Prepare for
landing." He put his thumb over one of

the buttons on the gadget at his waist and gradually lowered them both to the ground.

"So for once you *were* listening when Erika told us about our new gadget!" puffed Zoe, staggering as Ben released her from his grip. "I'm glad I had my backpack strapped on securely."

Ben flipped the far end of the EEL line off its branch, and retracted it. Then he looked up at the broken walkway dangling high above their heads.

"We've lost our prey," said Zoe crossly. "He'll be far away now."

"But at least we know what he was up to," said Ben grimly.

Zoe looked at him, puzzled.

"There's no way that was an accident," Ben said solemnly. "When the wood cracked I could see it had been sawn almost through – just ready to break with the weight of a person."

Zoe gasped. "He must have cut through the ropes as well."

"Those walkways were fine when we were here this afternoon," said Ben. "And I wonder if he had something to do with the explosions as well – whatever they were."

"Our mission's not going to be as straightforward as we thought." Zoe sounded worried.

"You're right," said Ben. "Someone's targeting the reservation." He had a sudden thought. "And maybe the booking cancellations weren't just a mistake. Do you think those loggers who scared off Kawan are behind it all?"

"Whoever it is," said Zoe, "I reckon it's someone who knows Mat."

"How can you be sure?" asked Ben.

"Mat said he takes the same route every day to call Kawan. Only Mat's friends and people who work with him will know that.

He would have stepped on the sabotaged walkway and fallen – without an EEL to save him."

"Do you think Mat realizes someone's after him?" asked Ben.

"If he does, he's not going to tell us, is he?" said Zoe. "He thinks we're just visitors."

Ben nodded. "We must speak to Mat about the walkway straight away."

"And admit we've been out on our own in the night?" scoffed Zoe. "How's that going to look?"

"You're right," agreed Ben. "He'll see it in the morning anyway."

Zoe suddenly bent down and picked up a silver strip of paper from the ground. She held it out towards Ben triumphantly.

"It's a chewing gum wrapper," said Ben with a shrug.

"And it could be a clue," replied Zoe.

"Whoever sabotaged the walkway must have dropped it just now."

"How d'you figure that out, Sherlock Holmes?" scoffed Ben. "It could have been here for days!"

"That's where you're wrong." Zoe grinned. "This wrapper's perfectly dry. It rained before we came out, so it must have been dropped after that. And who else would be out here in the middle of the night?"

"Good thinking!" exclaimed Ben. "You're not as dopey as you look."

Zoe slipped the chewing gum wrapper into her pocket. Then she rubbed her shoulders under the backpack straps and stretched painfully. "I thought you were going to pull my arms out of their sockets when we fell!"

"Sorry," grinned Ben. "I'll remember not to save your life next time!" He took his BUG and pressed some buttons to bring up the satellite map of the area. "Let's get back before it's light."

They set off, pushing through the undergrowth, but they hadn't gone far when Zoe suddenly went sprawling.

"Ow!" she groaned, rubbing her shin. "There's some sort of rock or something in those ferns."

Ben took a look and gasped. "I knew those explosive noises sounded familiar. We heard them all the time on that farm near Gran's cottage." He parted the leaves to reveal a small metal box. "It's a bird scarer."

"We saw how terrified Kawan was just now, and no wonder Lola and Kiki were looking so nervous earlier, if this thing has been going off every night. Someone is deliberately trying to frighten the orang-utans," exclaimed Zoe.

"For all we know, Kawan might have come back before, but been scared off each time," said Ben.

"I'm going to put a stop to it," said Zoe through gritted teeth, giving the box a hard kick. "Ow!"

"That won't do it," said Ben. He put his fingers under the edge of the metal cover and prised it open. Inside was a battery and a timer set to go off in the early hours. He wrenched the wires off the battery and put the cover firmly in place. He grinned at his sister. "Better than breaking your toes."

The birds' morning chorus filled their ears as the children crept back through the courtyard.

The air had become very hot and still. The minute they closed their door a sudden flash of light lit the bedroom. Thunder crashed overhead and a torrent of rain began hammering down like a deafening waterfall outside their window.

"We're back just in time!" said Ben. "Glad we didn't get caught in that!"

"I hope that despicable man did!" said Zoe, pacing up and down. "We have to find out who he is."

Ben gave a gaping yawn. "But not now." He lifted the mosquito net and flopped on to his bed. "Got to get a few more hours' sleep."

Ben dozed off almost immediately, but Zoe lay for a long time, imagining how terrified poor Kawan must be feeling right now. At last she fell into a troubled sleep.

CHAPTER EIGHT

"Daud, Talib!" Mat's distant voice broke through Zoe's dreams. She heard some words in Malay and slipped her translator into her ear. "Come quickly," she heard, "and bring your tools."

She gave Ben a shake, then pulled on long trousers and a T-shirt and put her BUG into her pocket. She crept out. Ben staggered along behind, blinking sleepily in the daylight. They hovered unseen in the doorway that opened on to the compound. Yasmin was standing barefoot amongst the

steaming puddles. She looked wide-eyed
and anxious as her husband ran up to her.
Biza clung to her neck, rubbing his cheek
against hers as if to reassure her.

"It's OK." Mat put his hand on her arm.
"One of the walkways has broken."

"He's found it already!" Ben whispered to
his sister. "Maybe now he'll begin to realize
there's something funny going on."

"It was probably the storm earlier," Mat
went on. "I am so thankful it didn't happen
when anyone was on it."

"Are you sure it was just the storm?"
sighed Yasmin. "We've had such bad luck
lately. Do you think it could be the loggers
from before?"

"They wouldn't dare," said Mat calmly,
as Daud appeared with the tools. "Try not
to worry."

He spotted the two children standing in
the doorway and came over. "I'm sorry, Ben

and Zoe," he said in English with a regretful smile. "I must make some emergency repairs to one of the walkways this morning. But I'll be back this afternoon, and I have a surprise for you. In the meantime, Yasmin will look after you."

He turned to Daud and told him what had happened in Malay. "Where's Talib?" Ben and Zoe heard him ask.

"He was chopping wood just now," said Daud. "I don't think he heard you call."

As he spoke, Talib sauntered round the corner behind him, carrying a pile of logs. A strange expression flashed across his face when he saw his employer.

"That's odd," muttered Zoe, as the two workers followed Mat into the forest. "Did you see how Talib reacted?"

"Probably annoyed that he's got some extra work," said Ben.

Mat's wife turned dejectedly towards the

door where the children were standing.

"Is everything all right?" Ben asked innocently, holding the door open for her to go through. "You all look so worried."

"Just a broken walkway," said Yasmin. She gave a weak smile and the children realized she didn't have her husband's cheerful, optimistic attitude to the recent events. "Would you like some breakfast?" She showed them through into the kitchen. "We have nasi lemak. That is rice boiled in coconut milk – it's quite delicious. But I must ask a favour. Could one of you hold Biza for me while I make it? He is such a naughty boy and stops me getting on."

Yasmin peeled the baby orang-utan off her and held him out.

"That's Zoe's territory!" Ben laughed. "Get ready for the oohs and aahs."

Zoe grinned and stepped forward. The little ape looked doubtful for a moment, but climbed slowly on to her shoulder. Zoe could feel his breath on her neck – and then his hand pulling her BUG out of her pocket! Zoe gave a cry and quickly snatched at it before it had made its way into Biza's mouth. As she tussled with his surprisingly strong hands and tried to block the shrieks in her ear she heard the sound of deep laughter from the doorway. Mr Ostrander came in, tucking his sunglasses into the top pocket of his shirt.

"You'll never get the better of Biza," he
said. "He rules the roost here. Isn't that
right, Yasmin?"

Yasmin looked up from the cooker.
"Morning, Pieter," she said with a smile.
"Yes, he may be the smallest but he's
definitely in charge." She waved him to
a seat. "You remember Ben and Zoe."

"Good to see you again," said Mr
Ostrander. He turned to Zoe, who was still
struggling to put her BUG back in her
pocket. "Be careful, or that little fellow will
make off with your pocket gamer thing –
and it looks too valuable to lose!"

Zoe grinned. If only he knew how
valuable her BUG was!

"I'm afraid you've missed Mat," Yasmin
told Mr Ostrander. "He's gone off to make
some repairs to one of the walkways."

"Storm damage?" asked the plantation
owner. "It was a fierce one last night."

"Probably," said Yasmin, putting the nasi lemak on to plates for the children.

Biza finally gave up the struggle for Zoe's BUG, dropped to the floor and made straight for Mr Ostrander's boot lace. Yasmin scooped him up. "Come on, you little devil. Time for your sleep."

"What have you two got planned today?" asked Mr Ostrander.

"Mat's prepared a surprise for us this afternoon," said Zoe.

"But we're not sure what's happening this morning as he's busy right now," added Ben.

"How big is your plantation, Mr Ostrander?" Zoe asked suddenly. "Do you know how many trees you have?"

"That's a difficult one!" Pieter Ostrander replied.

"And what size tractors do you use?" Zoe persisted. "Bet they're awesome!"

Ben stared at her, wondering why his

sister was suddenly interested in the details of oil palm farming.

"Tell you what," said Mr Ostrander with a smile, "as you're so keen to find out about my land, why don't you come and look for yourselves?"

Ben saw Zoe grinning at him. So that's what her plan was! She'd got them an invitation to the plantation. And it wasn't to count trees or look at tractors. Zoe was hoping they'd get a glimpse of Kawan and make sure he was all right.

CHAPTER NINE

Zoe and Ben stood at the prow of Mr Ostrander's speedboat, watching it cut through the brown water of the Munia River. They'd had a tour of the processing plant and been plied with food in a very posh dining room. Now they were off to see the fields of oil palms close up.

On the right bank were the rows of oil palm trees Mat had pointed out from the walkway. The rainforest trees of the reservation spread away to the left. They could hear the sound of distant hammering coming from somewhere among them.

"That must be Mat and his men seeing to the repairs," said Zoe. "They'll have to go and check the whole thing after that. It'll take ages."

"Here's that bend in the river we saw yesterday," whispered Ben. "We must be coming to Kawan's old territory."

"So beyond it is the reservation boundary and the new palm oil plants," said Zoe. "It's just coming into view now."

"This is near where Mat said Kawan had been spotted," said Ben. "Somehow we've got to have a look among those trees. But of course we can't just ask."

"Why not?" said Zoe. "We don't have to say anything about Wild, after all." Holding on to the safety rail, she made her way back to the cabin where Mr Ostrander was at the wheel.

"Has Mat told you about his missing favourite orang-utan?" Zoe asked their host.

"Ah yes, Kawan," said Mr Ostrander, looking serious. "Mat was cut up about him leaving the reservation. I know the little chap's been spotted among my trees – although I haven't seen him myself."

"Could we have a look there?" Zoe pointed ahead to where the land had been cleared and the ordered rows of small saplings were planted. "I'd just love to be able to say I've seen him – to reassure Mat

90

that he's still all right," she added quickly.

"Of course we can," said Mr Ostrander.

As the river curved to the right, he steered the speedboat to a small jetty on the left bank and cut the engine.

"As you can see, these are my newest trees," Mr Ostrander told them as they walked between the oil drums towards the more mature growth. "They'll be producing fruit for oil production in four years' time. I've increased my work force by ten per cent for these. Good for the local economy."

Ben looked at Zoe. He could guess what she was thinking. This was all very interesting, but they couldn't wait to get searching in the trees.

Mr Ostrander pointed over to a new red-roofed shed in the distance. "That's where the next crop of oil palm fruit will be stored. Then it will be taken to the processing factory."

His mobile phone rang. "Excuse me," he said, as he flicked it open. "Do have a look round. Let me know if you see Kawan."

Zoe and Ben didn't waste any more time. They chased off between the rows of seedlings until they reached the regimented lines of trees. Keeping the edge of the seedling patch in sight, they walked among the low hanging fronds of the oil palms, listening intently to the calls of unseen creatures. Ben held up his BUG and pressed some buttons. "I'm analyzing the cries," he said. "No orang-utan I'm afraid – just birds."

"Isn't that Talib?" said Zoe suddenly. "Over there, coming out of the little door at the end of the shed." She got her Wild binoculars out and zoomed in on a figure carrying a heavy can. "It is," she said in surprise. "What's he doing on Mr Ostrander's land? He's meant to be helping Mat repair the walkways."

They crept towards the tall, wooden shed, and peered round to see Talib stop for a moment. He put down the can, pulled something from his pocket and unwrapped it. He placed it in his mouth and began to chew, throwing the wrapper to the floor. Then he picked up the can again and sauntered off into the trees.

"Did you see that?" gasped Zoe. She ran and picked up the silver wrapper. "This is just like the one I found beneath the walkway last night. Do you think it was Talib who sabotaged the walkway?"

"What was he carrying?" muttered Ben. "Let's take a look inside the shed."

They slipped inside and found themselves in a small tool store at the end of the main shed. Rakes, spades and machetes hung on the walls. A dirty old tarpaulin had been thrown in one corner. Ben pulled it back to reveal four more cans identical to the one Talib had taken. He picked it up and heard liquid sloshing inside.

"It's petrol!" gasped Zoe, sniffing at it. "But why would Talib be stealing petrol?"

"If you're right about the gum," said Ben, "then Talib is Mat's enemy. It was Talib who sabotaged the walkway and put the scarer in place. And now I've got the awful feeling he's going further. He's planning to set fire to the reservation!"

CHAPTER TEN

Mr Ostrander chatted away pleasantly as he drove Ben and Zoe back to the Adilah Reservation. The children sat in the back, trying to answer as if nothing was wrong.

Ben remembered the strange expression on Talib's face when Mat told him about the broken walkway. He must have been surprised that Mat was still in one piece. Ben needed to find out more about Talib. Perhaps Mr Ostrander could help, but how could he bring up the subject without it looking suspicious?

"Shame there was no sign of Kawan," Mr Ostrander was saying sympathetically.

"I expect Mat will keep looking," said Ben. "And his staff," he added with a sudden flash of inspiration. "We know that Daud's very fond of him."

"But we don't know about Talib," Zoe burst in, catching on. "He's very quiet. Do you know what he's like, Mr Ostrander?"

"I don't know Mat's men very well," said the plantation owner. "Which one is Talib?"

"Older than Mat, with greying hair," Ben told him.

"Surly chap?" Mr Ostrander shrugged. "Never spoken to him." He swung the jeep through the gates of the reservation.

Mat was waiting for them in the courtyard.

"Just in time for your surprise treat," he beamed, as Mr Ostrander's car disappeared in a cloud of dust. "I'll let you go and freshen up first. Meet you here in five minutes."

Back in their room, the children turned to each other anxiously.

"Our surprise couldn't have come at a worse time," said Ben.

Zoe nodded. "What are we going to do about Talib? He could start the fire at any moment. We must tell Mat."

"We can't," said Ben. "We'd have to tell him about the walkway and the shed. He mustn't know we've been investigating. Anyway, how do we know he'd believe us?"

"Then we'll call Uncle Stephen." Zoe pulled out her BUG and pressed the hot key that would put her in direct contact with Wild HQ.

"Greetings!" They heard their godfather's sleepy voice. It was the middle of the night on his island. "Any news of Kawan yet?"

"We've seen him," said Zoe. "But there's much more to tell."

"Worse than I thought," said Uncle

Stephen, when Zoe had finished her report. "Erika's in North Borneo. I'll get her to alert the authorities right now – anonymously, of course. They'll be on their way at once. They take fire in the forest very seriously."

"And as soon as the threat's over we'll try using the call again to lure Kawan back to his old territory," added Zoe. "There's no bird scarer to keep him away now."

"You go and enjoy your surprise," said their godfather. "And leave everything to me."

"Are you ready?" they heard Mat calling from the courtyard. They swung their rucksacks on to their backs and headed outside to find him standing by a small, open-top jeep. He grinned. "Hop in!"

"Where are we going?" asked Zoe, as Mat steered them down a bumpy track. It was impossible to see ahead because of the dense trees.

"You'll see in a minute."

The jeep turned a corner and in front of them was a cleared area, about the size of a football pitch, leading to a runway. Ben and Zoe could see it was a small airstrip, and then they spotted the craft shimmering in the heat in the middle of the tarmac.

"A balloon!" gasped Ben. "Fantastic!"

Zoe gave a whoop of delight. "Double fantastic!"

"It's the best way to see the rainforest." Mat beamed. "Ready for a little ride?"

They walked towards the balloon, which was still being filled with hot air.

"Perhaps our surprise hasn't come at the wrong time after all," Zoe murmured to Ben.

Ben frowned. "How d'you work that out?"

"If a fire did start, at least we could see exactly where it was and put out an alert immediately!"

Whoosh! Mat turned up the flame that burned under the huge red balloon envelope. A man untied the rope tethers and Ben and Zoe felt the basket rise up into the air.

"It's a bit bumpy!" yelled Zoe, over the noise of the roaring flare.

"You'll get used to it." Mat smiled.

They were soon at the height of the treetops. Mat pulled on a cord.

"This opens the parachute valve a little," he told them. "Don't worry, we're not jumping! It just lets out hot air to stop us gaining any more height. Can you feel the tug on the basket? At different heights the winds travel in different directions. We've reached a patch of wind that's blowing south-eastwards. Just what we need to go over the reservation."

"And if we have to change direction we just go up or down to catch a different wind," said Ben.

"You've got it!" said Mat. "I can't guarantee to get us back in the centre of the tarmac, but I've never missed the airstrip yet."

Above the forest canopy the air felt fresher, and Ben and Zoe could feel a welcome breeze on their skin. Parrots glided over the treetops below them, their bright wings flashing through the air.

"This is all the Adilah Reservation," said Mat, proudly gesturing over his land.

The tops of the tallest trees reached out but didn't quite touch each other. Small trees filled the gaps below. It looked like an endless sea of green.

"Some of the trees are seventy-five metres tall," explained Mat. "All sorts of creatures live up there: monkeys, spiders, snakes, lizards."

Zoe screened her eyes. "What's that mountain over there?" she asked, as she looked at a barren peak far in the distance.

"Mount Kinabalu," said their guide. "You'll have a good view now we're so high." He handed them binoculars.

"I don't like the look of the dark clouds over it," said Ben, focusing on the mountain. "Are we going to get wet?"

"They're a long way off," Mat told them. "Don't worry, we should be back before it rains. I'm turning to take you right across the reservation. We're at the south-eastern point here. You can see the oil palms stretching away at the edge of my land."

"There are the seedlings," said Zoe. "It looks like a join-the-dots puzzle from here."

"We have to get higher," said Mat, turning up the flame. "Hopefully we'll pick up a helpful wind to take us north now."

"This is sure to bring the tourists in," said Ben. "You'll be so busy, you'll be recruiting more staff."

"Maybe," laughed Mat. "I'll manage with

Daud and Talib for the moment."

Zoe caught Ben's eye. "Have they worked with you for long?"

"Daud and I were at school together," Mat told her. "Talib works for Mr Ostrander – has done for years. Pieter's lent him to me for a short while. He suggested I'd need more help with the reservation opening up for visitors and sent him over." He stepped to the other side of the basket to check the balloon's position with his map.

"I don't understand," Ben hissed in Zoe's ear. "Mr Ostrander said he didn't know Talib."

Despite the heat Zoe felt a chill run up her back. "Why would he lie?" she whispered back. "He's a friend of Mat's."

Ben suddenly grasped Zoe by the shoulders, his fingers digging into her skin. "That's what he wanted us to think. But don't you remember – Mat said Mr

Ostrander wanted to buy Adilah when he first bought his plantation. It all makes sense now! When Mat wouldn't sell up he decided to get it another way."

"So you think Ostrander's the one behind the cancellations, the broken walkway and scaring off the orang-utans – and probably the logging that frightened Kawan away, too?" said Zoe in a shocked whisper. "All that stuff about helping Mat was just a cover. He sent Talib to work for him and secretly carry out his horrible plans."

"How clever." Ben nodded. "Ostrander appeared to be a hero when he had the loggers chased off. But I bet he'd sent them there in the first place. All the time he's been trying to make sure that the reservation fails. I suppose he's intending to step in as soon as it does and nobly buy the land off Mat."

At that moment the flame above them

puttered and flickered. Mat turned the ring
on one of the propane cylinders and
frowned. "It's run out of gas. I thought I
asked for them *all* to be filled." He shrugged.
"I expect the other two are OK." He quickly
opened the valve on another cylinder, but
there was no burst of fire from overhead. Ben
and Zoe could see that Mat was beginning to
look worried. "I don't understand it," he
muttered. "I told Talib to top
them up – and the gauges
are showing full."

"Talib?" shouted Zoe. "Talib filled the cylinders?"

Ben quickly knelt down by one of them. A tiny blob of chewing gum had been squeezed in under the needle.

"Look inside the glass!" he shouted. "He's used his gum to wedge the gauge so it shows full."

Mat twisted the third valve open, beads of sweat breaking out on his forehead. "This one's the same. They've been tampered with! Why would Talib do this?"

The children stared at him, white-faced. Over their heads the flame spluttered – and died. Horrified, Ben and Zoe felt the wind throbbing in their ears as the balloon began to drop through the air, gaining speed. The sides of the nylon envelope, no longer filled with heat, flapped loudly in the downward rush and the dense green of the forest below raced up to meet them.

"Get down as low as you can!" shouted Mat above the din. "Brace yourselves for the impact. With luck we'll hit the canopy and our fall will be broken."

Ben and Zoe could see how close they were to the open land of the oil palm plantation. If they crash-landed there, they didn't stand a chance.

CHAPTER ELEVEN

Zoe gave a shriek as she felt the basket smash down on top of the trees, throwing her against Ben. All around was the deafening crack of breaking branches. The basket tumbled down through the canopy, almost flinging Ben over the side. Zoe grasped his arm and hauled him back in. They clung together, huddled in one corner of the basket.

Suddenly the basket gave a huge jolt and came to rest at a crooked angle, swinging from side to side, the balloon envelope tangled in the branches above.

"We've stopped falling!" gasped Zoe, hauling herself up by one of the ropes.

Ben peered out. "The balloon's caught on a tree. We're safe – for the moment."

"But look at Mat!" Zoe edged her way slowly over to where their pilot lay in a crumpled heap.

"Is he alive?" Ben clambered round to join her, making the basket rock dangerously.

Zoe felt his pulse. "He's unconscious," she said, hearing the worry in her own voice.

"He must have been knocked out."

Ben pulled out his BUG. "I'm going to call Uncle Stephen," he said. "He can get help—"

He gave a cry as some of the balloon fabric ripped and the basket fell to the branch below.

"There's no time for that," said Zoe urgently. "We've got to get down to the ground now."

"We can use our EELs," said Ben. "I'll take Mat."

Zoe pressed the button on her EEL belt. As she leaped out of the basket, she felt the cord fasten to the branches above.

Ben gripped Mat tightly round the waist and prepared to jump. He knew he had to get them clear of the basket, which was starting to rock dangerously. They couldn't risk getting trapped as it fell and dragged down to the ground. Then the EEL wouldn't be able to work. But Mat was like a dead weight in his arms. Ben couldn't move him at all.

There was a crack of snapping wood and the basket broke loose from the tree. Ben felt himself being thrown into mid-air. He clung to Mat for all he was worth as they plummeted. Heart in his mouth, he hoped they weren't too heavy for the EEL. Then, to his relief, he felt the jerk of the cord.

As soon as Mat was safely down on the ground, Zoe felt his pulse. "It's very fast," she said, worried. "And he looks so pale."

"We need to get him medical help as soon as possible," said Ben. "I'll contact Uncle Stephen now."

The chugging sound of a quad bike burst through the trees.

"Someone must have seen the balloon come down!" he exclaimed. "Help's arrived!"

"And they've got transport," said Zoe excitedly. "They can take Mat to hospital! We're over here!" She jumped to her feet and waved her arms.

But the next instant their hope turned to dread as the quad came into view.

Their rescuer was no rescuer at all. It was Pieter Ostrander.

He cut the engine, dismounted and came over to them. Out of the corner of her eye Zoe saw Ben's fingers reaching for his BUG. *Surely Ben's not going to try and alert Uncle Stephen*, she thought. *It's too risky.* But just in case, she ran forward to Mr Ostrander to block his view.

"Thank goodness you're here," she cried. "There's been an accident and Mat's hurt."

"I saw the balloon come down," said Mr Ostrander in a concerned tone that now rang falsely in the children's ears. "I came as quickly as I could. What a dreadful accident."

He strode over to Mat. Mat's eyes flickered open.

"No accident," he groaned. "Talib did this … your man…"

"Oh dear," said Pieter Ostrander. His voice was suddenly hard as he gazed down at Mat. "If you hadn't worked that out I might have rescued you and carried on playing the supportive friend. But now I can't let you live to tell your tale. It won't fit in with my plans at all."

A look of utter disbelief spread over Mat's face. Ben and Zoe stood in stunned silence. They hadn't guessed the lengths to which Mr Ostrander would go to get his hands on the reservation.

At that moment, an ear-splitting chirruping noise filled the air. Zoe saw Ben's BUG drop to the floor and the slight movement of his foot as he kicked it under a bush. They couldn't call Uncle Stephen, so Ben was doing the only thing he could think of. But how could Kawan help them?

Mr Ostrander started at the loud call. He pulled a gun from his pocket.

"What's that noise?" he demanded.

"Must be a bird," said Ben, trying to keep his breathing calm. "Scared by the quad bike."

Mr Ostrander lowered his gun. "You should thank me really," he said with a chilling smile. "You're going to be famous. It will be in all the papers tomorrow that Mat and two young tourists were killed in a tragic ballooning accident."

"But we haven't been," said Zoe defiantly.

"Everyone will think so, Zoe. And there'll

be no evidence because a forest fire is going to sweep through the reservation."

Keeping the gun trained on them, he pulled some lengths of rope out from the pocket of his jacket. He strode over to Mat, who stared at him in disbelief. "The rope will burn away. There'll be no evidence of what I've done."

"I thought you were a friend, Pieter," Mat managed to whisper.

Ostrander laughed coldly. He laid the gun beside him and yanked Mat's hands behind his back.

Zoe began to edge away.

Pieter Ostrander raised an eyebrow. "Stay still, Zoe. I would *prefer* not to shoot you as bullets will survive the fire. But I will if I have to. And I won't miss. I'm a very good shot."

"But if you start a fire, it might burn your oil palms," called Zoe desperately.

"I have thought of that, Zoe," said

Mr Ostrander. "The wind's not in that direction. Talib and I checked that most carefully." He looked at his watch. "In fact he'll be starting the fire now."

There was a sudden shrill shriek above his head. Pieter Ostrander looked up in horror to see a furious blur of orange fur hurling itself at him.

"It's Kawan!" yelled Zoe.

The next second the orang-utan had sent Mr Ostrander sprawling. The gun spun out of his grasp.

Lips curling in a snarl, the angry animal turned and picked it up.

"Let it go, Kawan," came Mat's gentle voice. "Throw it away."

With a sharp cry Kawan raised the gun high over his head. Then he smashed it against a tree trunk, again and again. At last he slung the useless weapon away into the undergrowth.

Next, Kawan advanced on his enemy. Terrified, Pieter Ostrander shuffled back on his elbows and scrambled to his feet. He stumbled to his quad bike and roared away.

Kawan watched him go. Then he threw back his head and gave a deep, hollow call. Creatures all around took up the cry and for a few seconds the canopy was alive with harsh howls and squawks. Then the orang-utan turned back to stare at the children.

"Hope he isn't going to think *we're* his enemies too," said Zoe, not daring to move. "After all, we were there when he was frightened off last night."

But Kawan showed no sign of fear now. He squatted next to Mat, stroking his head. Mat roused himself and focused on his friend.

"Good boy," he said in a faint whisper. "Brave boy."

"We need to get out of here," said Zoe, "before Talib starts the fire." She went up to Mat and untied the ropes.

Out of sight of Mat, Ben reached for his BUG. Uncle Stephen needed to know the danger they were in. He was just pressing the Wild hot key when he heard a frightened shout.

"Ben!" cried Zoe. "I can smell smoke. The fire's coming."

CHAPTER TWELVE

"Hello!" came Uncle Stephen's voice.

"Ostrander's trying to sabotage the reservation!" Ben yelled into the BUG. "He's burning the forest – and we're in it!"

"I've worked out your position using your signal," came back Uncle Stephen's voice immediately. "The fire's east of you. Head away from it – as fast as you can!"

Holding his good arm, Zoe forced Mat to his feet. "You're coming with us!"

With her help, Mat painfully staggered a few paces, then swayed and leaned heavily on her shoulder. Ben came and supported Mat's other side.

Kawan gave a low, anxious cry and set off. Then he stopped and turned, and chattered at them urgently.

"He's heading for the plantation and he wants us to follow," exclaimed Ben, surreptitiously checking the map on his BUG. "He's staying on the ground. He must know we can't climb into the trees."

They moved as fast as they could, half carrying the injured Mat between them. Roots and vines threatened to trip them with every step. Above their heads, they could see wind was disturbing the tops of the trees. It was blowing towards them as they ran.

"At least the wind's not blowing the fire our way," said Zoe through gritted teeth.

But as they went, the smell of burning suddenly grew stronger and they tasted acrid smoke on their tongues. Ben and Zoe found themselves taking shallow breaths to keep from choking. They could hear Mat's ragged gasps as he forced himself along. The trees above were filled with alarmed cries and scrabbling noises as animals fled their homes. Kawan urged them on with loud calls.

"Spoke too soon," gasped Zoe. "The wind's changed direction."

She suddenly pitched forwards as her foot caught in a thick, twisted buttress root. She landed in the middle of a brightly coloured plant. The fleshy leaves parted, showering her with water and insects.

"Can you feel how hot it's getting?" She gasped as she scrambled to her feet. She turned to look behind her and raised a wobbly finger, pointing at the orange light flickering in the distance. "See the glow!" she said in a horrified whisper. "The fire's coming!"

They plunged on in their desperate flight. Crack! A terrible sound filled the smoky air, followed by another.

"Trees exploding!" yelled Ben. "We've got to move faster."

The black smoke was making it almost impossible to catch their breath. As the temperature soared, the sweat poured into their eyes, blinding them. Ben wiped his hand across his face. Behind them the flames were licking at the sky.

Kawan stopped as they came to the edge of the plantation. Ahead of them were the regularly-spaced oil palms. He turned and chattered anxiously, urging them on.

But Mat pulled back.

"Can't go that way," he panted weakly. "Oil palms burn really fast!"

"No choice," croaked Ben, pulling him along a corridor of trees. "No way back."

Now their ears were filled with spluttering, sizzling sounds as trees and shrubs were engulfed in a relentless wave of flame.

Like vicious wasps, red-hot embers showered down on them. The children flailed at the burning patches, scorching their hands. Kawan was giving frightened little cries as the sparks fell on to his fur.

Zoe's mouth felt full of ash and the heat was hurting her lungs. She glanced at Ben's soot-streaked face. He was in no better shape. And Mat was hardly dragging one foot in front of the other now.

But she knew they couldn't stop. The fire had reached the oil palms. If they'd thought it had been moving fast before, it was nothing to how it gobbled up these trees.

As they pushed their way through the undergrowth, Mat collapsed to the ground. The children knelt down and tried to pull him to his feet, but he felt like a dead weight in their arms. Kawan came to his side, keening softly.

"Got to keep going," cried Zoe, her voice choking. "We'll be burned alive!"

"You go on," Mat croaked.

Then, all of a sudden, the sound of the roaring flames changed. Ben dashed away another spark and found his hand was wet. Not wet with damp, sooty sweat, but clean water. He looked up. All he could see was a swirl of thick, dark smoke. But he felt drops of water pounding on his face.

He grabbed Zoe's arm, giving her a shake. "Got a chance!" he managed to get the words out through his parched lips. "It's raining!"

CHAPTER THIRTEEN

The next morning was bright and sunny.
The smell of yesterday's fire still hung heavy
in the air. Bird and monkey cries could be
heard in the canopy. Ben and Zoe stood on
the walkway, in the middle of Kawan's
territory, looking out towards the river.

"Listen to that racket," grinned Ben.
"It's as if nothing happened."

"It's amazing that this part of the
reservation was spared from the flames,"
said Zoe. "If that rainstorm hadn't come
when it did..." She looked down at her

bandaged hands. The burns were painful, but it could have been a lot worse. Her BUG beeped and she read the incoming text.

"Erika says she'll be coming for us this afternoon," she told Ben.

"It's a shame we can't stay to help Mat," he said. "He has such a lot of extra work to do now. He's lost about a quarter of his trees."

"Did I hear my name?" came a voice.

They turned to see Mat slowly making his way along the rope walkway, Yasmin – and Biza – hovering anxiously behind.

"He must have finished with the police at last," whispered Zoe.

The police had questioned the children first. Ben and Zoe had pretended to be frightened tourists, but they were able to give a lot of details about Mr Ostrander.

"I've brought the rusks!" Mat said cheerfully.

He steadied himself on the rope handrail. Like Ben and Zoe, he had burns on his hands. "I've had trouble keeping them from this cheeky little ape here!" He pulled the bag out of his pocket and gave one to the baby orang-utan.

"Any sign of our friend?" asked Yasmin.

Ben and Zoe shook their heads.

"Kawan's a hero now," said Mat. "We've had telephone calls from all over the world, television and radio, all wanting to hear about the amazing rescue and how he led us away from the fire."

"And the best part is," added Yasmin, "it has given us a lot of publicity. We've had people getting in contact wanting to know how they can help support the reservation. A computer firm in Japan want to sponsor my next balloon and we've even had a student from America asking if he can spend his gap year here!"

"But you've lost a lot of trees," said Zoe.

"It's true," said Mat. "But within a week, there will be shoots springing up. Dormant seeds that have been waiting for the chance, lying quietly under the cover of the other trees. It will take time, but it will all grow again. We're going ahead with all our guest bookings."

"And do you think most of the animals are safe?" asked Ben.

Mat nodded. "They're much better than us at sensing danger."

"And the police have put out a warrant for Pieter's arrest," Yasmin told them. "Though how they got to know about him so quickly is a mystery."

Ben and Zoe caught each other's eye. Somehow Uncle Stephen always got his messages through to the right people.

"And Talib's confessed everything," said Mat soberly.

He looked searchingly at Ben and Zoe. "When I was hurt," he said, "I thought you had some special machine and were calling Kawan with it."

Ben and Zoe glanced at each other. What could they say? Then Zoe grinned. "You must have been delirious," she said kindly. "You'd been knocked out in that balloon, after all."

"Of course," said Mat, to their relief. "How ridiculous!"

The branches in a nearby tree swished and Kawan appeared.

"Here he is!" said Zoe. She tried to make the chirruping noise, but it sounded more like a squawk.

"Let me try!" Ben rolled his tongue and made a very good imitation of Mat's calling sound.

"Impressive!" said Mat. "You only heard it once or twice."

Kawan jumped down on to the walkway in front of them. He regarded them solemnly. Mat handed the paper bag to Zoe.

"If you would oblige," he said.

Zoe removed a rusk and held it out. With a low, soothing moan, Kawan reached out a long arm and took it in his fingers. He sniffed it for a moment, and then began to nibble at the edges.

"He's being very polite!" laughed Ben.

Kawan stared at him as he ate. Then he froze, his eyes glued to something over Ben's shoulder. He pulled back his lips and gave a warning screech that made Ben and Zoe jump. A loud chattering began behind them. They turned to see Biza clambering on to Yasmin's shoulder, catching at her hair. He looked terrified.

Ben grinned. "I think Kawan's telling Biza

that this is his territory, and he wants him out of it!"

"I think he's saying something to us all," said Zoe.

"What's that?" asked Mat.

"It's obvious." Zoe smiled. "He's saying, 'I'm home'."

ORANG-UTAN SURVIVAL

Orang-utans are only found in the wild on the islands of Borneo and Sumatra. In the last ten years it is thought that their numbers have declined by up to 50%.

No. of orang-utans living wild today	fewer than 60,000
No. of orang-utans on Sumatra	about 6,000
No. of orang-utans in the wild in 1900	about 315,000

Life span: about 45 years in the wild
Oldest orang-utan recorded: 58 years old

The name orang-utan
is Malay and means
"man of the forest".

Male orang-utans are
approximately twice the size of
females. In the wild males
weigh between 175 and 225
pounds, but males in captivity
can reach 300 pounds or more.

Females usually only have
one baby at a time. The young
stay with their mothers for
longer than any other primates
except humans. They
are finally independent at
about 7-8 years old.

STATUS: ENDANGERED

The Bornean orang-utan is on the red list of the International Union
for Conservation of Nature, who say that its numbers are decreasing.
The Sumatran orang-utan is critically endangered on that list.

RESCUE

ORANG-UTAN FACTS

THREATS

LOSS OF HABITAT

The biggest threat to orang-utans is the loss of their rainforest home. Tropical rainforests are being cut down for timber and the land is being cleared for oil palm plantations and mining. Orang-utans have lost 80% of their habitat in the last 20 years! Forest fires, deliberate and accidental, also destroy their habitat.

KILLED AS PESTS

Orang-utans are occasionally killed as pests by plantation owners and farmers.

LOW REPRODUCTON

In the wild, a female orang-utan only gives birth every 7-8 years. She usually has up to four surviving offspring in total.

Orang-utans are highly intelligent. They poke twigs into holes to catch insects, and use sticks to test the depth of water before entering it. Some use leaves as umbrellas, as gloves to protect their hands, or even as cushions in spiny trees!

PREDATORS

Humans, clouded leopards, tigers and possibly the Asian hunting dog are all dangers to orang-utans.

THE ILLEGAL PET TRADE

Mother orang-utans are killed and their infants sold as pets.

It's not all bad news!

In spring 2009 scientists discovered a large population of orang-utans, possibly more than 2,000, in the remote jungles of Borneo. Conservationists now need to work with local authorities to protect the area.

On reserves like the Tanjung Puting National Park the orang-utan can live and breed in relative safety. Some (non-government) conservation groups in Borneo are talking with oil palm companies about schemes in which land will be set aside for privately owned nature reserves.

Twins Ben and Zoe are devastated at being left at home when their parents head to Africa for their next veterinary adventure. But they're about to have an adventure of their own. Contacted by renowned zoologist Dr Stephen Fisher, they are recruited into Wild. Soon the children are on their way to Sumatra to rescue a tiger and her two cubs from a gang of vicious poachers...

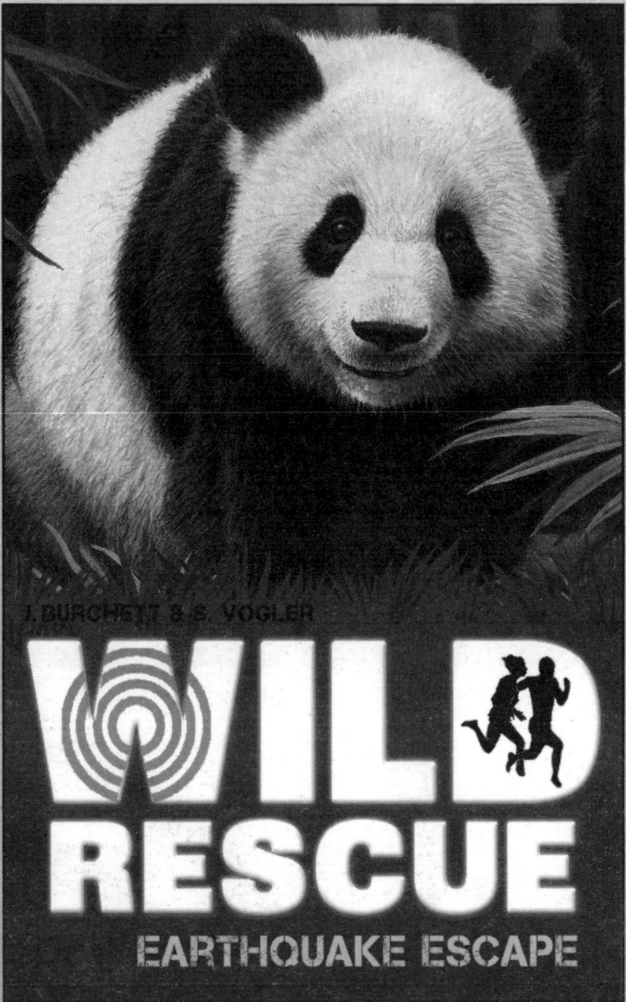
J. BURCHETT & S. VOGLER
WILD
RESCUE
EARTHQUAKE ESCAPE

Following a massive earthquake, an orphaned giant panda has escaped from a sanctuary in China's Sichuan Province. Not only is he at risk of attack from leopards, but it seems he may have strayed into an area where all the bamboo has died. With the panda cub now in danger of starvation, it's up to Ben and Zoe to rescue him.

Following reports of a polar bear found dead near an Alaskan village, Uncle Stephen is sending Ben and Zoe to investigate. It is highly unusual for the animals to be found so close to human habitation. But the mission takes another turn when they learn that the dead bear had recently given birth. This means there are orphaned cubs out there. Will Ben and Zoe find them in time?

If you want to find out more
about orang-utans visit:

www.orangutan.org.uk
www.savetheorangutan.org.uk
www.orangutan.org
www.wwf.org.uk